This book belongs to:

....

Based on the episode "Paddington and the Ice Skates" by Holly Lamont

Adapted by Lauren Holowaty

First published in the United Kingdom by HarperCollins *Children's Books* in 2022
HarperCollins *Children's Books* is a division of HarperCollins*Publishers* Ltd
1 London Bridge Street
London SE1 9GF

www.harpercollins.co.uk

HarperCollins*Publishers*
1st Floor, Watermarque Building, Ringsend Road
Dublin 4, Ireland

1 3 5 7 9 10 8 6 4 2

ISBN: 978-0-00-849793-4

Printed in the United Kingdom by Bell and Bain Ltd, Glasgow

Based on the Paddington novels written and created by Michael Bond

MIX
Paper from
responsible sources
FSC
www.fsc.org
FSC® C007454

FSC is a non-profit international organisation established to promote the
responsible management of the world's forests. Products carrying the FSC
label are independently certified to assure consumers that they come
from forests that are managed to meet the social, economic and
ecological needs of present and future generations.

Find out more about HarperCollins and the environment at
www.harpercollins.co.uk/green

The Adventures of Paddington™

The Ice Disco

HarperCollins Children's Books

Dear Aunt Lucy,

This week I've learned that we
shouldn't let our worries hold
us back.
It all began when I stumbled upon
something strange in the park . . .

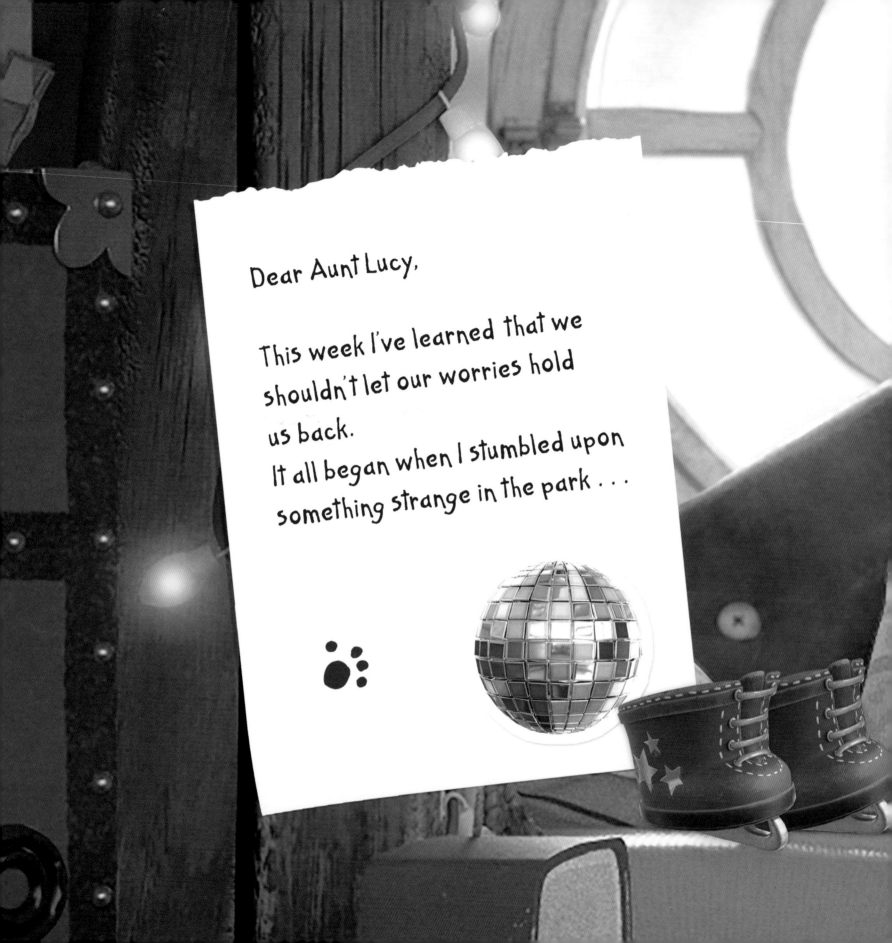

One day, Paddington saw something he'd never seen before – an ice rink!

"Wow!" he gasped in amazement. "Oh, good morning, Mr Gruber!" he said, waving at his friend on the other side.

"Good morning, Paddington," said Mr Gruber sadly, before walking off.

Paddington wondered what was wrong. He stepped on to the ice to speak to him. "Oh, Mr Gruuuuu . . ."

". . . berrrrr!" cried Paddington, as he slipped and slid on the shiny surface.

"WOAAAAHHH!"

Luckily, Ms Potts caught him.

"Thank you, Ms Potts!" said Paddington, struggling to stay on his feet.
"Whatever this is, it's very slippy!"

"It's an ice rink," Ms Potts explained. "It's *meant* to be slippy! I'll order
you some special bear-sized skates so you can join in at the ice disco
on Friday."

"Oh, I would LOVE to go to an ice disco!" said Paddington.

Back at the Browns' house, Jonathan and Judy were about to go to the ice rink to practise their routine with Mateo.

"Hold it!" called Mr Brown. "Jonathan, your shoelaces are undone *again*!"

"Oh, Dad! We're in a hurry!" grumbled Jonathan, quickly tying his laces.

"Oh, do you think we might have a dance on the ice?" Mrs Brown asked Mr Brown.

"All that slipping and falling?" said Mr Brown. "Oh no, you won't get me on the ice!"

But, after Mrs Brown left, Mr Brown told Judy and Jonathan that he was going to teach himself to skate to surprise Mrs Brown. "How hard can it be?" he said.

Skating was *much* harder than Mr Brown thought! He wibbled and wobbled everywhere.

"AHHHH!" he gasped, almost doing the splits.

"You're doing great, Dad!" said Judy.

Jonathan, Judy and Mateo practised their routine and Jonathan did
an amazing final jump.

"Woohoo!" they all whooped. They were ready!

Later, at Mr Gruber's shop, Paddington was admiring some red ice skates.

"Why are you selling those magnificent skates?" Paddington asked.

Mr Gruber explained that he was a professional ice skater when he was younger, but he'd had a bad fall and hadn't skated since.

"Well, now's your chance!" said Paddington.

"No, no – it's *too* late now. I'm *too* old," sighed Mr Gruber, and he put his skates in the shop window.

Paddington couldn't wait for his bear-sized ice skates to arrive so
Mr Gruber took him to the park to practise his balancing skills . . .

"OOOH!"

His sliding skills . . .

"AHHH!"

And his speeding skills!

ZOOOOOM!

Mr Gruber was impressed. Paddington was going to make a wonderful ice skater!

A few days later, Paddington came racing into Mr Gruber's shop with a box containing his new skates. But when he opened the box, he found **roller skates** *not* ice skates.

"Oh no!" said Paddington. "These won't work on the ice rink!"

Just then, the shop's doorbell rang . . .

DING!
DONG!

It was Mr Curry.

"I'd like to try those skates on," he said, pointing to the red skates in the window.

"No, you can't!" said Mr Gruber, holding them tightly. "I mean . . . I don't think I can part with them. Sorry."

Mr Curry harrumphed, "I will never shop here again!" But seconds later he changed his mind. "Oo! How much for the porcelain bunny rabbit?"

"Are you keeping your skates so you can use them at the ice disco?" asked Paddington after Mr Curry had left.

"No, it is not *I* who will be skating in them," said Mr Gruber. "With some changes, I think we could make them fit . . . you!"

"Fit me?" said Paddington with surprise. "Oh, it would be an honour to wear them!"

It was the night of the ice disco and the rink was packed. But the last person Mrs Brown expected to see was Mr Brown!

"Have you really learned to skate just for me?" she asked, as he offered her his hand.

"I'm doing it! I'm really skating!" he cried, clinging tightly to Mrs Brown's shoulders as he shuffled along.

Meanwhile, Mr Gruber helped Paddington put on his brand-new bear-sized ice skates. They fit perfectly!

"I cannot believe the progress you have made in such a short time, Paddington! Now, go and enjoy the disco!" said Mr Gruber.

"Oh, thank you, Mr Gruber," said Paddington, as he glided on to the ice.

"Welcome to our first ice disco," announced Ms Potts over the microphone. "Now, please clear the ice as we have a special performance by The Ice Extravaganzas!"

The crowd cheered as Judy, Jonathan and Mateo skated across the ice together.

Swissshhh! Swooooshhh! Whooooshhh!

Everything was going to plan until Jonathan was about to do the final jump . . .

"Jonathan!" shouted Mr Brown. "Laces!"

But it was too late. Jonathan tripped, his ice skate flew off his foot and he began to spin out of control . . . "WAAAAAAH!"

Paddington leaped on to the ice to help Jonathan but together they started to spin faster and faster!

Jonathan spun off safely to the side of the rink, but Paddington just kept whirling round. He was about to crash when . . .

suddenly Mr Gruber caught
him by the paw and helped
him skate to safety.

"PHEW!"

Paddington and Mr Gruber then twirled and glided over the ice, doing a beautiful ice dance together. When they stopped, the crowd cheered.

"Thank you for saving me, Mr Gruber," said Paddington.

"Thank you for saving *me*," said Mr Gruber. "Because of you I can once again enjoy ice skating – one of my life's greatest loves. You really are **a rare sort of bear.**"

It seems there's really nothing better than learning a new skill or refinding one you thought you'd lost. I do wish you could've seen Mr Gruber, Aunt Lucy. He looked spectacular!

Love from,
Paddington